First published in the United States in 2015 by
Eerdmans Books for Young Readers,
an imprint of Wm. B. Eerdmans Publishing Co.
2140 Oak Industrial Dr. NE
Grand Rapids, Michigan 49505
P.O. Box 163, Cambridge CB3 9PU U.K.

www.eerdmans.com/youngreaders

Originally published in Israel in 2013 under the title
Just Like I Wanted
by Kinneret, Zmora, Dvir Publishing House,
10 Hahagana St., Or Yehuda 60212, Israel
www.kinbooks.co.il

Manufactured at Tien Wah Press in Malaysia

21 20 19 18 17 16 15   9 8 7 6 5 4 3 2 1

Library of Congress Cataloging-in-Publication Data

Keller, Elinoar, author.
Just like I wanted / by Elinoar Keller and Naama Peleg Segal;
illustrated by Aya Gordon-Noy.
pages cm
Summary: As she tries to create a perfect picture, a girl keeps
drawing outside the lines but rather than give up, she simply
transforms the picture into something new.
ISBN 978-0-8028-5453-7
[1. Stories in rhyme. 2. Drawing — Fiction. 3. Persistence — Fiction.]
I. Peleg-Segal, Naama, author. II. Gordon-Noy, Aya, illustrator. III. Title.
PZ8.3.K274Jus 2015
[E] — dc23
he 2014048075

FSC
www.fsc.org
MIX
Paper from
responsible sources
FSC® C012700

JUST LIKE I WANTED

Written by Elinoar Keller & Naama Peleg Segal

Illustrated by Aya Gordon-Noy

Translated from the Hebrew by Annette Appel

EERDMANS BOOKS FOR YOUNG READERS

GRAND RAPIDS, MICHIGAN • CAMBRIDGE, U.K.

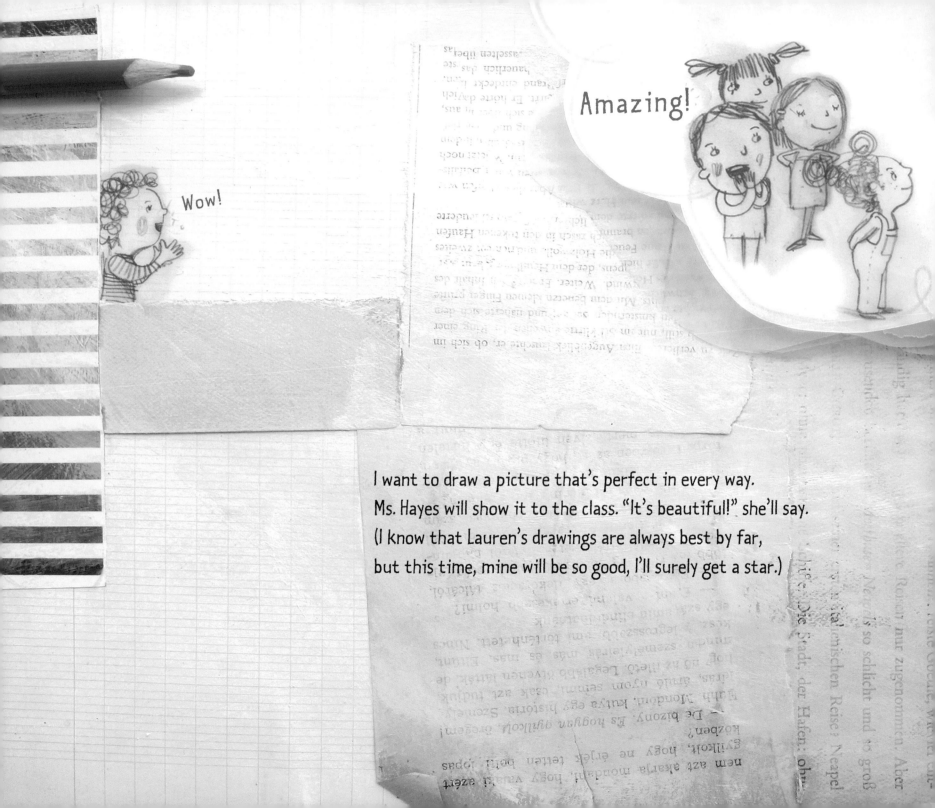

I want to draw a picture that's perfect in every way.
Ms. Hayes will show it to the class. "It's beautiful!" she'll say.
(I know that Lauren's drawings are always best by far,
but this time, mine will be so good, I'll surely get a star.)

I'll draw a girl who's clean and neat.
She wears a pretty dress.
She always knows just what to say.
She never makes a mess.

I'll draw her playing the piano.
Its keys shine black and white.
It's hard to color in the lines.
I have to get it right.
I try to pay attention.
The crayon's in my hand.
The first key's black, and then comes white.
Back to black and . . .

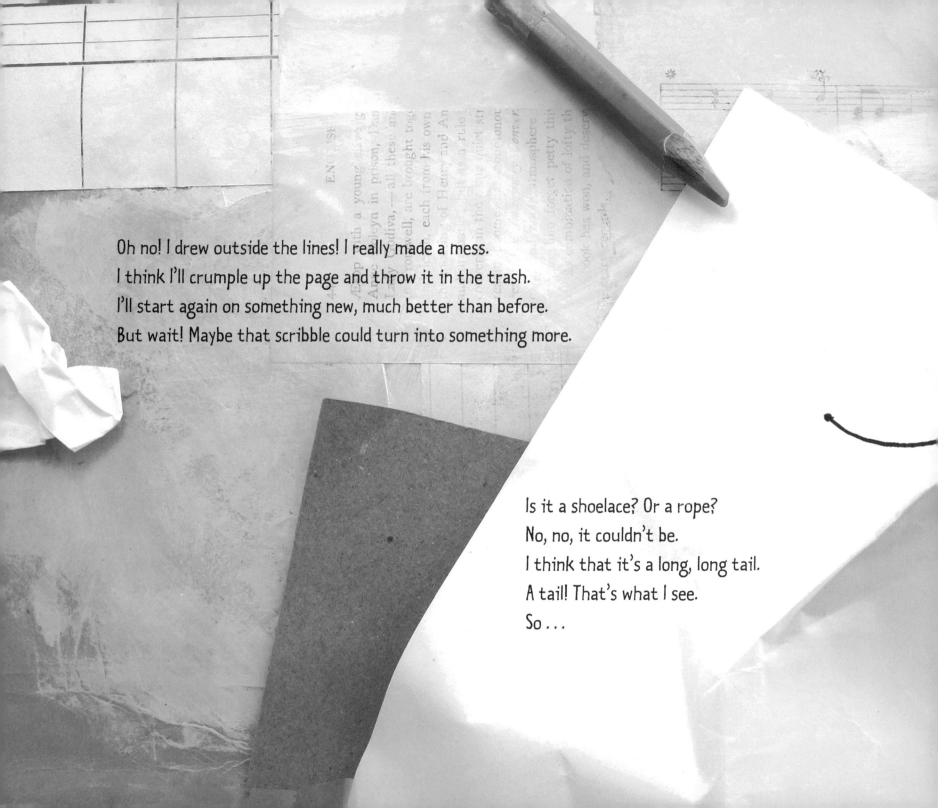

Oh no! I drew outside the lines! I really made a mess.
I think I'll crumple up the page and throw it in the trash.
I'll start again on something new, much better than before.
But wait! Maybe that scribble could turn into something more.

Is it a shoelace? Or a rope?
No, no, it couldn't be.
I think that it's a long, long tail.
A tail! That's what I see.
So . . .

It's not a piano. It's a horse! Yes, can't you see?
It's a horse! Off he gallops, fast and wild and free!

The girl takes a ride as she sits on his back.
She's an excellent rider. She stays right on track.
Together they gallop to the country of dreams.
A land full of candy and chocolates and cream.

The horse grabs at candies to take on the way.
A hundred! A million! He'll be snacking all day.

But how will he carry the sweets that he takes?
I know! I'll draw pockets for candies and cakes.
One pocket is plaid, one has stripes thick and thin.
And one has a zipper to keep pop rocks in.
I color with care, but my hand begins to wiggle.
Not this time! I'm trying so hard not to scribble . . .

Awww!

That makes me so mad! Why can't I stay in the lines?
Should I rip up this picture and begin one more time?
I will really miss the horse. I truly loved him so.
But with that scribble on his back, he surely needs to go.

Wait! I'll turn the line into a wing, and draw it on a plane.
Yes! An airplane in the sky. I'll start to draw again . . .

tweet

The horse is gone, and now a plane is way up in the sky.
The girl sits in the pilot's seat. She smiles as she flies by.

The birds all chirp their greetings. She answers right away.
The little girl can understand just what they want to say.
She soars up to the clouds and then she looks below.
The people look so tiny. They cheer and wave hello.

Suddenly an eagle comes, soaring way up high.
What's he doing here? I think. Why is *he* in my sky?
I think he's kind of scary. His feathers are black as night.
He has pointy teeth inside his beak. Watch out! He just may bite.

I'll color in the eagle with my crayon, dark and black.
It's pretty easy. He's so big. I color very fast.
But now I'm getting to the edge. I'd better take my time.
I'm trying to be careful and stay inside the lines . . .

What ? Not again . . .

Naughty line! You bad, bad line. Now what will I do?
I think it will become a ship. I'll draw a pirate, too.

Ahoy! There in the corner. Sailing way up high.
(Not every ship sails on the sea. This one floats through the sky.)
The pirate's very angry. He shouts and yells out loud:
"Who in the world can I rob up here above the clouds?!"

His face is red with anger. He waves his sword around.
I color in his wooden leg, hoping he'll calm down.
Another line is out of place! This time it's just as well.
I'll make that pirate disappear. I won't have to hear him yell . . .

I'll take apart the airplane.
The girl will get the wings.
I'll put her up upon a cloud,
a blue and puffy swing.
She is having so much fun.
She's happy as can be.
And I am feeling happy too.
Because the drawing was made by me!

I'll show my picture to Mom and Dad.
They'll be so proud of me.
Ms. Hayes, Lauren, and my class
will certainly agree.

I drew such a pretty picture.
Look and you will see.
It turned out just exactly
like I wanted it to be!

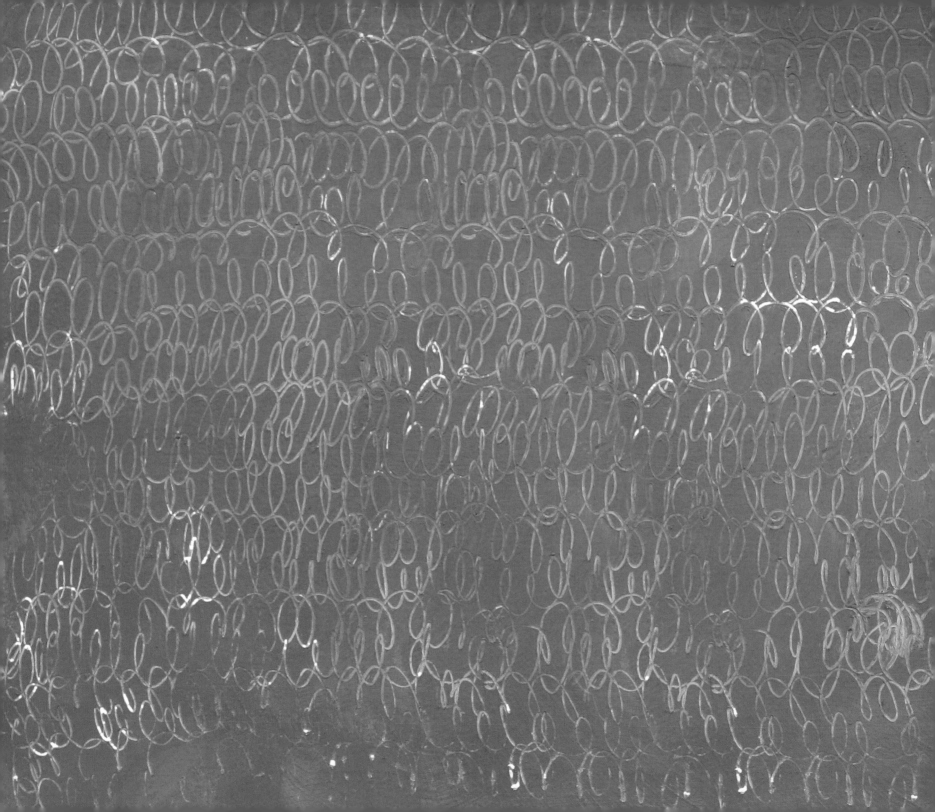